Topsy and Tim Go on an Aeroplane

By Jean and Gareth Adamson

Illustrations by Belinda Worsley

A catalogue record for this book is available from the British Library

Published by Ladybird Books Ltd
A Penguin Company
Penguin Books Ltd., 80 Strand, London WC2R 0RL, UK
Penguin Books Australia Ltd., 707 Collins Street, Melbourne, Victoria 3008, Australia
Penguin Group (NZ) 67 Apollo Drive, Rosedale, North Shore 0632, New Zealand

017

© Jean and Gareth Adamson MCMXCV
Reissued MMXIV

ISBN: 978-1-40930-057-1
Printed in China

www.topsyandtim.com

This Topsy and Tim book belongs to

_____

Topsy and Tim were off on their summer holidays.
They were going in an aeroplane.

The airport was very big.
Topsy and Tim had a long ride in a
bus to reach the terminal building.

Then they had a long ride on an escalator to get to the right part of the building.

Their luggage went for a long ride
too, on a moving platform.

Topsy and Tim watched an aeroplane land.
It looked much bigger when it was not in the sky.
The door was high off the ground.
"How will the people get out?" asked Topsy.

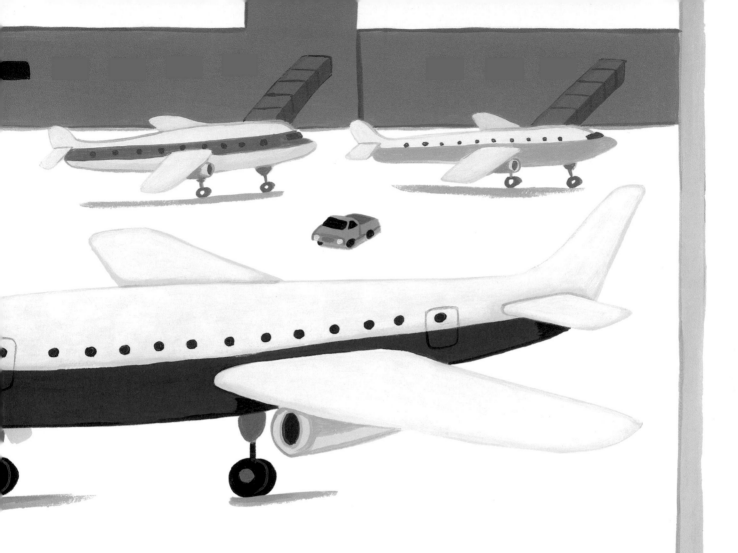

"Through a special tunnel," said Mummy. "You will see when it's our turn to get on the plane."

The loudspeaker voice announced that Topsy and Tim's aeroplane was ready. Soon they were walking along a telescopic tunnel and stepping into the aeroplane. It looked like a very long bus.

"Welcome aboard," said the
stewardess to Topsy and Tim.

The stewardess helped Topsy and
Tim fasten their safety belts.
She gave them some comics
and some sweets.

"Suck a sweet when the aeroplane starts to fly,"
she said. "It will stop your ears hurting."
Tim took two sweets.
"One for each ear," he said.
The stewardess laughed.
"They go in your mouth,
not your ears!" she said.

The big aeroplane flew up into the sky.
Topsy and Tim watched trees and houses grow as
small as toys.
"My ears have gone funny," said Topsy.
"You didn't suck your sweet, that's why," said Tim.

Topsy and Tim were flying above the clouds.
"Isn't this exciting!" said Mummy.
But the clouds went on for miles and miles.
Topsy and Tim began to fidget.

Lunch came in interesting plastic trays.
Each piece of food had its own shaped space like
the pieces of a jigsaw puzzle. Topsy and Tim tried to
swap pieces. The stewardess had to clear up the mess.
Then she said, "Topsy and Tim, the pilot would like
to talk to you."

The stewardess took Topsy and Tim to the pilot's cabin.
"Hello twins," said the pilot. "I've been hearing about you."
He showed Topsy and Tim all the switches and levers and
dials he used to fly the aeroplane.
"Do you think you could fly my aeroplane?" asked the pilot.
Topsy and Tim were not sure.

They went back to their seats and fastened their safety belts once more. Then they pretended to be pilots. "Will you land our aeroplane now, please, pilots?" asked the stewardess.

Topsy and Tim could see the flaps moving in the
aeroplane's wings to make it fly lower.
"I'm doing that when I move this lever," said Tim.
But Topsy and Tim both knew the real pilot was doing it.

Topsy and Tim's aeroplane landed with hardly a bump.

"Goodbye everybody," said Topsy and Tim.
They waved goodbye to the stewardess and to the
pilot up in the aeroplane's nose. Then they went to
meet their luggage on another moving platform.

Soon Topsy and Tim were
playing on a sunny holiday beach.
A big aeroplane flew across the sky.
"That's our plane going home," said Tim.
Topsy and Tim waved to their aeroplane
– and they thought it waggled its
wings back at them.

*Now turn the page and help
Topsy and Tim solve a puzzle.*

Topsy and Tim are looking down from the aeroplane.
They are trying to spot these things:

- two red tractors
- one church
- two windmills
- three horses

Can you spot them, too?

A Map of the Village

farm

Topsy and Tim's house

Tony's house

Kerr house

park

garage

health
centre

post
office

church

primary school

nursery school

police station

Have you read all the Topsy and Tim stories?

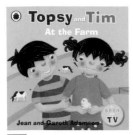 **Topsy and Tim** At the Farm — Jean and Gareth Adamson

☐ 9781409303367

 **Topsy and Tim** Go Camping — Jean and Gareth Adamson · seen TV

☐ 9781409303336

 **Topsy and Tim** Go on an Aeroplane — Jean and Gareth Adamson · seen TV

✓ 9781409300571

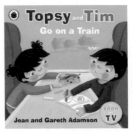 **Topsy and Tim** Go on a Train — Jean and Gareth Adamson · seen TV

☐ 9781409304241

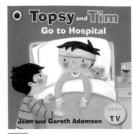 **Topsy and Tim** Go to Hospital — Jean and Gareth Adamson · seen TV

☐ 9781409304234

 **Topsy and Tim** Start School — Jean and Gareth Adamson · seen TV

☐ 9781409300830

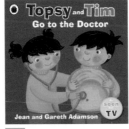 **Topsy and Tim** Go to the Doctor — Jean and Gareth Adamson

☐ 9781409303343

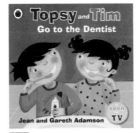 **Topsy and Tim** Go to the Dentist — Jean and Gareth Adamson · seen TV

☐ 9781409300588

 **Topsy and Tim** Have a Birthday Party — Jean and Gareth Adamson · seen TV

☐ 9781409300618

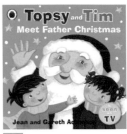 **Topsy and Tim** Meet Father Christmas — Jean and Gareth Adamson · seen TV

☐ 9781409311591

 **Topsy and Tim** Meet the Police — Jean and Gareth Adamson

☐ 9781409308836

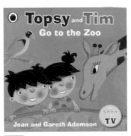 **Topsy and Tim** Go to the Zoo — Jean and Gareth Adamson · seen TV

☐ 9781409300847

 **Topsy and Tim** Meet the Firefighters — Jean and Gareth Adamson · seen TV

☐ 9781409307211

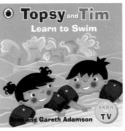 **Topsy and Tim** Learn to Swim — Jean and Gareth Adamson · seen TV

☐ 9781409300601

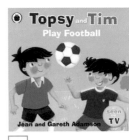 **Topsy and Tim** Play Football — Jean and Gareth Adamson · seen TV

☐ 9781409303350

 **Topsy and Tim** Safety First — Jean and Gareth Adamson · seen TV

☐ 9781409308829

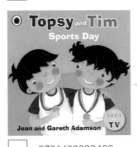 **Topsy and Tim** Sports Day — Jean and Gareth Adamson · seen TV

☐ 9781409309468

 **Topsy and Tim** Have Itchy Heads — Jean and Gareth Adamson · seen TV

☐ 9781409307204

 **Topsy and Tim** The New Baby — Jean and Gareth Adamson · seen TV

☐ 9781409300564

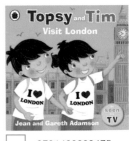 **Topsy and Tim** Visit London — Jean and Gareth Adamson · seen TV

☐ 9781409309475

 Available on the App Store

The Topsy and Tim app is available for iPad, iPhone and iPod touch.

It is also available on Android devices.